In a Pickle

JANEEN BRIAN

Illustrated by Bettina Guthridge

 sundance

Published by
Sundance Publishing
234 Taylor Street
Littleton, MA 01460

Copyright © text Janeen Brian
Copyright © illustrations Bettina Guthridge
Project commissioned and managed by
Lorraine Bambrough-Kelly, The Writer's Style
Designed by Cath Lindsey/design rescue

First published 1998 by
Addison Wesley Longman Australia Pty Limited
95 Coventry Street
South Melbourne 3205 Australia
Exclusive United States Distribution: Sundance Publishing

ISBN 0-7608-3285-4

Printed In Canada

CONTENTS

CHAPTER ONE

GOING BROKE

I'd never seen my nonna cry before. I didn't know what to do.

My name is Dominic, Dom for short, and I live with my Nonna Rosa in Cranwell. It's a small country town. Nonna Rosa has a great muffin shop on the main street. We live in the back part of the shop.

Two months ago, the Highway Department opened a freeway that detoured the traffic away from our town. Fewer and fewer people stopped for Nonna's homemade muffins. Nonna's business was failing.

Nonna Rosa was really worried. She only had the shop and a small pension to support her and me.

"We'll have to sell, Dominic," she sniffed one night.

But who would buy the shop now?

"What can we do?" I said to my best
friend, Rob.

"You'll have to do something that's really
eye-catching if you want people to turn off
the freeway and come into town," said Rob.

"Like what?"

"I don't know. A statue of a big muffin or something."

"Like the 'Big Pineapple' or the 'Big Lobster'?"

"Yeah."

"Good idea. But a muffin?"

"Okay, okay. It might not look that impressive. What else does your nonna make?"

"Apart from muffins, just tea and coffee."

"A big teacup?"

We both shook our heads.

CHAPTER TWO

FOR THE BIRDS

Nonna Rosa's eyes looked red and swollen again.

"We have to do something, Nonna," I said. "If the shop closes down, we lose our home. What then? Where do we go? And I'd probably have to go to another school."

I dreaded coming home from school each night.

"Toss these to the birds," Nonna Rosa would say, grimly. The birds would feast on leftover bran muffins, cherry muffins, and apple and blueberry muffins.

Nonna needed to bake in case people did come in. But, on the days when just a few people came, she could only freeze so many leftovers. The rest were wasted.

One day, Steve, from down the road, told us he was selling his gas station to a big company. If that wasn't bad enough, the company was going to build a bigger place, and serve fast food. There'd be video and pinball games, too.

SCALE:

"They're crazy," said Nonna Rosa. "It won't work. People won't pull off the freeway."

But the building started. Rob came home with me after school each day, and we'd check out what had been done.

The day of the grand opening came.

"You should see the signs on the freeway," said Nonna Rosa. "They're enormous!"

"See, Nonna," I said. "People will come in now. We'll be all right."

But it didn't work out like that. Most of the people simply went to the gas station, and I still had to give the leftover muffins to the birds.

CHAPTER THREE

WITH DINOSAUR JELLY

One day, Janey came home with Rob and me. We were doing a group project on food.

"My favorite subject," Janey grinned.

Nonna Rosa brought us a plate of muffins and jam and some orange juice. We began to plan our project.

"Yum," said Janey, licking the jam off her fingers, "these muffins are great!"

"Hey!" I cried. "I know something we could do. We could do a project on how to save Nonna Rosa's business."

Rob and Janey looked at me like my brains had been sucked out by a vacuum cleaner.

But I was excited. "That's about food!"

Janey stalled. "Well, it would be different,"
she admitted finally.

"But not exciting," said Rob.

He was right. That's the whole problem. Nonna Rosa's muffins were great—but they weren't exciting.

How can you make muffins more exciting? Make them with dinosaur jelly? Potato peelings? Marshmallow and broccoli?

"Your nonna's a good cook," said Janey. "Couldn't she make something that would sell better?"

"Like what?"

"Like hamburgers!" said Janey.

"They already sell them at the gas station," I sighed.

"They're precooked," said Rob. "Make yours different."

"How? Hamburgers are hamburgers."

"Put different things on them," said Rob.

Our project was getting nowhere.

CHAPTER FOUR

PICKLE PROBLEM

Nonna Rosa listened to our idea.

"Pizza, lasagna, spaghetti—fine, but hamburgers? I've never made them before," she said.

"What do you put on them?"

"Tomato, lettuce, onions, sauce, pickles . . ."

"Pickles?" repeated Nonna, thoughtfully. I looked at her curiously.

"Have I told you about Nonna Shapira's famous pickle recipe?" she asked.

"Not that I remember," I said.

"Tell us," drooled Janey.

"Well, her pickles were famous, believe it or not, because of a movie star. He was visiting our city, and Nonna Shapira left him a jar of her pickles at the hotel as a present. The movie star loved them, and he wrote a letter to Nonna Shapira telling her how good they were. Nonna Shapira was tickled pink!"

"They must've been good," said Rob.

I grabbed Rob. "That's it! Nonna could put Nonna Shapira's famous pickles on the hamburgers!"

Janey shouted, "Yes! We could write that in our project, too!"

Nonna sighed. "It sounds like a good idea," she said, "but I don't know how to make them."

"Nonna," I cried, "there must be a recipe somewhere." She didn't look hopeful.

"I'll help you find it," said Janey. "I love looking in recipe books."

"That's the trouble," said Nonna. "Nonna Shapira hid her pickle recipe before she died. It's somewhere in the house. I've looked and looked, but I've never found it."

That was the end of that. We went back to the project.

"I can't think of anything else," said Rob.

"Are there secret doors in this house?" asked Janey, her mind still on the hidden recipe.

I shook my head.

"What about under the floorboards?" inquired Rob.

I groaned. Imagine trying to look under them!

I shrugged. "I don't know where it could be."

"Let's look anyway," said Janey.

"Might as well," said Rob. "This project is going nowhere."

"I'll look in my room," I said. It was such a mess that I didn't want Janey to see it.

PRIVATE

keep OUT!

THAT MEANS YOU

We split up and started searching. Janey looked behind furniture. Rob looked behind pictures.

I pulled up the carpet under my bed. After a while it got boring.

"Keep looking," urged Janey.

We looked in drawers. We looked in closets and in old coffee cans and behind chair cushions.

Rob found an old piece of candy and a dollar bill—but no recipe.

I went looking for Nonna to tell her. She was holding a pile of bills in her hand, and she was just staring at them. "Nonna Shapira always had money to pay her bills," she sighed.

Then she grinned wickedly. "Do you know where she kept her money?"

I shook my head, not really interested.

She pointed to the wall where three statues of china birds "flew" toward the ceiling. "In back of that small one!" she said.

We all laughed.

Then I cried, "Nonna! Do you think . . . ?"

Rob and Janey looked at me.

Nonna knew what I was thinking. Her hands shook as she took the smallest bird off the wall. She slid two fingers into the hole and pulled out an old piece of paper. It was rolled up. We held our breath.

Could it be?

She opened it. The writing was faded, but the heading read "Pickle Recipe."

"Hoorah!" we shouted.

"Now what?" said Nonna, smiling.

"Start making pickles!" I cried.

CHAPTER FIVE

CONTEST OR NOT

The next day at school we had another idea. Rob, Janey, and I asked our teacher, Mr. Simons, if we could hold a contest.

"It's about food," said Janey, trying to sell him on our idea.

"Tell me what your plans are," he said.

Fortunately, Mr. Simons liked our idea.

We decided to hold a jingle contest at school. Kids could make up a jingle about Nonna Rosa's hamburgers and famous pickles. The winner would get a coupon for twenty free hamburgers!

Kids started writing songs. They made up funny poems. They practiced raps. All for Nonna Rosa's hamburgers!

Rob and I made a big sign advertising "Nonna Rosa's Hamburgers," and we put it on the freeway near the exit sign for our town. We called the local radio station, and we also invited everyone we could think of to come on Saturday.

Nonna Rosa got busy. The house reeked of onions and vinegar! I helped make hundreds of hamburger patties, and the butcher let us put them in his freezer.

On Saturday morning, Janey and Rob came over. We were cutting up rolls and making salad when Nonna Rosa came in. Her face was all puckered, and she looked angry.

"Have you seen it?" she asked.

"Seen what?" we all said, puzzled.

"The sign at the gas station." Nonna Rosa's voice shook. "Anyone who buys gas today gets . . . a free hamburger."

"No!" I cried.

"That's not fair!" shouted Janey.

I wanted to go and give the owner a piece of my mind. I gritted my teeth. "We'll still have the contest," I said.

"No one will buy our hamburgers," said Nonna Rosa. "Why should they when they can get one free at the gas station?"

I racked my brain. "They *will* buy ours," I cried. "We'll just be extra busy, that's all."

The other kids looked puzzled.

CHAPTER SIX

WINNERS ALL

At noontime there were a lot of kids and grown-ups in the shop. Jill Cross, from the radio station, was going to judge the jingle contest.

"Let's start!" I said to the others.

First, Janey introduced Brian and Jimmy, on guitar. Then Pam and her sisters sang. Janey's brother and his friends did a rap. Froggy did the sounds of a robot eating his first hamburger. That cracked us up.

After six more acts, the contest was over.

Jill Cross announced that Brian and Jimmy had won with their jingle, "The Hamburger Bugs."

Jill and all the contestants celebrated with free hamburgers.

"Mmm," said Jill, "that's the best hamburger I've ever tasted. What's on it?"

Nonna Rosa told her about Nonna Shapira's famous pickle recipe.

Jill made some notes and said it might make a good story for her radio program.

When I told her where we'd found the recipe, she laughed. She was so easy to talk to that I ended up telling her about what was happening to Nonna Rosa's business, and how we might have to sell it and leave town. And I pointed to the free hamburger sign at the gas station.

"That must make it hard for you," she said.

I agreed. Then I told her about the *other* sign I'd put up on the freeway.

"It might be working already," she said, smiling, as several cars pulled up.

"Is this where you get a free muffin with every Nonna Rosa Hamburger?" asked one driver.

"It sure is," I said, and winked at Nonna Rosa.

"Every day for the next month!" she added, pleased with her idea.

I handed Rob and Janey some paper plates.

"The jars of jam are in the kitchen," I said. Let's do it!"

"Slave driver," replied Rob, with a grin.

So that's how people got to know about Nonna Rosa's Hamburgers. Now we don't have to give away free muffins. People come from all over for them—but they especially come for Nonna's hamburgers with the famous pickles. Nonna Rosa sells hundreds of bottles of those pickles.

In fact, the whole house smells of Nonna Shapira's pickles!

Sometimes Nonna Rosa's eyes still get red—but now it's because she's been cutting up so many onions!

Janeen Brian

Janeen learned to love words and reading when she was a very young child. By the time she was eight years old, she had already decided to become a teacher.

As an adult, Janeen became a teacher-librarian and the mother of two daughters, and she began writing. Janeen has done all kinds of writing—books, poetry and verse, fiction and nonfiction, plays and scripts, and stories, poems, and plays for children's magazines. She also has acted with a professional children's theater group and has done dozens of television commercials and narration for videos.

Janeen owns a border collie named Nell. She lives in a seaside city in South Australia, not far from where she grew up.

ABOUT THE ILLUSTRATOR

Bettina Guthridge

Bettina Guthridge grew up in Australia. After studying art and teaching for three years, she moved to Italy with her husband. Ten years and two children later, Bettina and her family returned to Australia where she began illustrating children's books.

Bettina has illustrated many books for children—books written by well-known children's authors such as Ogden Nash and Roald Dahl. Her first picture book, *Matilda and the Dragon*, was followed by *Hurry Up Oscar*.

Bettina has had two successful exhibitions of sculptures made from objects she found on the beach. Her special pet is a border collie named Tex.